LITTLE DOG SNIFF

AND

THE TWINS

LITTLE DOG
SNIFF
and
THE TWINS

by

GERALDINE FOSTER SMITH

Illustrated by

ROBERT HENNEBERGER

1955   E. P. DUTTON & CO., INC.   *New York*

FOR

HELEN

MY GOOD FRIEND

CONTENTS

LITTLE DOG SNIFF

AND

THE TWINS

THE LITTLE BLACK DOG

It was late afternoon, and Ricky walked slowly down the road. The road was a very little one that went this way and that way, now near a brook, now under tall trees until finally it joined the highway that led to the city.

Ricky was very unhappy. Just a little while ago, his twin brother Roddy had said he would never play with him again. All because Ricky had borrowed Roddy's favorite baseball without permission and had forgotten to put it away when he was through with it. That would have been bad enough, Roddy said, but a puppy came along and found the ball and chewed it to bits. Mother saw him from the upstairs window, but before she could get down to rescue the ball, the puppy had done his worst.

That was why Roddy had got mad and had said he would never play with Ricky again. And Rod always meant what he said. So Ricky was running away. He wasn't going to live in the same house with a twin who wouldn't play with him.

Soon Ricky came to the place beside the brook where he and Roddy always had such good times together. It was shady and cool there, and Ricky was very hot. He sat down on a big stone. In a minute, he kicked a small stone with the toe of his shoe. *Plop* went the stone into the water. Then Ricky kicked another stone, and it went *plop,* too. But he wasn't having any fun. Nothing was going to be any fun any more.

"I want Roddy to play with me again," he said aloud in a very sad voice. "And I want a dog. If I had a dog, I wouldn't be running away. Because my dog wouldn't let any little old pup come into our yard and do things like chewing up Rod's ball.

"And if I had a dog, he would play with me even if I was bad," Ricky went on. "He'd like me no matter what I did."

Up in a tree, a bird began to sing. Ricky sat very still. In a moment the little bird stopped singing, then flew down to a stone in the middle of the brook. Then he began to sing again. He looked so comical, sitting there on the stone, singing away, that Ricky couldn't help laughing. At that, with a *cheep,* the bird flew up into the tree again.

Ricky took off his shoes and socks and started wading out into the brook. The water felt ever so good on his hot feet, and he tried jumping from stone to stone.

"Ricky!"

"Ricky!"

"Hi, Ricky!"

Ricky stopped still. It was Roddy, coming through the woods.

"Hi, there, Ricky," Roddy shouted again, rushing out from the trees.

Ricky jumped for another stone, missed it, and sat down with a splash in the water.

Roddy didn't even notice. "Look what I've got, Ricky," he cried. "Look!"

Ricky looked, then stared in surprise. Yes, it was true! Roddy had a little black dog in his arms.

"Where did you get him, Rod?" he asked breathlessly. Then, jumping to his feet and rushing out of the brook to his twin's side, he begged, "Let me hold him, Roddy. Please let me hold him."

Roddy handed the little dog to his dripping twin. "I found him at Joe's garage. I went down there looking for you, and just when Joe was telling me he hadn't seen you since yesterday when you were there with Daddy getting the tire fixed, up ran this little dog."

Roddy stopped to scratch the little dog behind his ears. Then he went on, "Joe said it was the same little Scottie that was at the garage when he opened up this morning. And I liked him right away. I guess he liked me, too, because he began to wag his tail as soon as I spoke to him."

"Where did he come from?" Ricky asked.

"Joe doesn't know," answered Roddy. "He thinks probably someone stopped by to get gas early this morning before the garage was open. And the little dog must have jumped out of the car without the owner's noticing."

"Is Joe going to keep him if the owner doesn't come back?" asked Ricky.

"No, he isn't," replied Roddy. "He has a dog. And what do you think? He said if no one came after the dog before he closed up tonight, he was going to take him to Mr. Mike at the Police Station. Then I asked Joe if we could look after him today. And Joe said yes. And he told me that if anyone came asking about a little lost dog, it would be easy to call our house about it."

All the time that Roddy was telling his story, Ricky was holding the little black dog tightly in his arms. Now he put the puppy down on the ground. In a flash, the little dog headed for the water, waded in, and sat down.

"He saw me doing it and now he is doing the same thing," cried Ricky in delight.

Both twins laughed. And Roddy said, "You sure

are wet, Ricky." Then he held out his hands and called, "Come here, little dog. Come here, good little black dog."

The little dog stood up, waded to the edge of the brook, sprang out, and, running over to the twins, shook himself thoroughly.

"He's drier now than you are, Rick," said Roddy. "I guess we'd better go home."

16

"Yes," agreed Ricky, "and ask Mother if we can't keep him."

"We can't keep him if someone comes to Joe's after him," said Roddy.

"Here's hoping nobody does come," replied Ricky, and, drying off his feet and legs as best he could, he started to put on his shoes and socks.

With one sock and shoe on, he looked up at Roddy. "Do you think Mother will let us keep him if nobody comes for him?" he asked.

Roddy looked down at the little black dog, and the little black dog looked up at him. "W-e-l-l," he said slowly, "maybe she will, but we'll have to ask Daddy, too."

"Oh," said Ricky, putting on the other sock and shoe slowly.

As if he knew what they were saying, the little black dog now ran first to one twin, then to the other. And his little tail went wag, wag, wag.

Ricky reached down to pat him, then said, "I'm sorry about your ball, Rod. I'll buy you a new one out of my allowance. But you will play with me again, won't you?"

"Sure I'll play with you," Roddy told him. "And you don't need to buy me a new ball. I still have my old one and it's good enough."

Ricky laughed happily. My, it felt good to know that he and Roddy would go right on having good times together. Having even better times, that is, for now they would have a little black dog. Somehow he was sure they were going to keep him.

As the three of them went down the street toward home, Roddy and Ricky whistled their favorite tune. And the little black dog's tail went wag, wag, wag all the way.

DO THE TWINS HAVE A DOG?

When the twins came to a red house with white shutters, they turned in at the walk, for that was home. Right at their heels, the little dog followed after them.

"Mother," shouted the boys. "Mother, come quick and see what we have."

Mother threw open the front door, exclaiming, "What is it this time, boys?"

"A dog!" cried the twins. "A little black dog. May we keep him?"

"Just a minute!" laughed Mother, coming down the porch steps. "Let's begin at the beginning. Where on earth did you get so wet, Ricky?"

"In the brook," replied Ricky. "But about this little dog, Mother, he—"

"I was looking for Ricky," broke in Roddy, "and I went to Joe's garage to see if he'd been there. Joe said no, Ricky hadn't, and then this little dog came running up."

"He's been around Joe's all morning," said Ricky. "And Joe thinks he's lost."

"Joe says he probably jumped out of a car when the owner stopped at the garage early this morning," added Roddy. "And Joe thinks the owner never noticed that his little dog was gone until he was too far away to come back."

"And, Mother," said Ricky, "Joe has a dog and he doesn't want another. He was going to take this one to Mr. Mike at the Police Station, if no one came for him today. So I said we'd look after him because it would save Joe and Mr. Mike all that bother. So here he is."

Mother smiled and patted the little black dog's

head. "I see," she said. "And he is a cute little Scottie. But—"

"Joe said he'd send anyone here who came looking for him," interrupted Roddy. "So it's all right for now, anyway."

"I'll tell you how I got so wet," said Ricky, hastily. "I was jumping on some stones in the brook when Roddy called me. And I was so surprised I slipped and sat down right in the water."

"And when I came up, this little dog waded in and sat down, too," said Roddy. "It was awfully funny."

"I'm sure it was," agreed Mother. "Now then, go upstairs as fast as you can, Ricky, and put on dry clothes."

Ricky didn't move. "I've just got to know if we can keep this little dog if no one comes after him," he said.

"So do I," said Roddy.

"Don't set your hearts on no one's coming for him," Mother told them. "He is a well-cared-for little dog, someone's pet, I'm sure. Anyone can see he isn't a stray. Probably right now a little boy or a little girl who loves him very much is looking everywhere for him."

"But we love him, too, Mother," Ricky told her. "And he loves us. Look at his tail wag. Please say we can keep him."

Just then the little dog barked, "Yap!"

"See," said Roddy, "he's saying he wants to stay with us."

Mother laughed. "More likely he is telling us he is hungry. Roddy, you take him into the kitchen and give him a bowl of milk. And you, Ricky, do as I said and get dry clothes on. You are dripping!"

So Roddy took the little black dog into the kitchen. Just as he was filling a bowl with milk, in ran Penny, the twins' small sister.

"O-o-o-o-o-oh!" she squealed. "Look at the darling little dog. Is he ours?" And she sat down on the floor beside the small visitor. The little dog sniffed Penny's hand, then licked it. Penny laughed and took him in her arms.

"We have a dog," she chanted. "We have a dog. We have a dog."

"He isn't really ours, Penny," explained Roddy,

as he put the bowl of milk down on the floor. "Joe at the garage is letting us look after him until his owner comes for him."

Penny hugged the little dog so tightly he couldn't get away for his milk. "But I want him," she declared. "I want to keep him always."

"I know what," she said suddenly, letting the little dog go free. And she hurried from the kitchen, and up the front stairs.

2 4

The little dog ran straight for the milk, drinking it down so fast it was all gone by the time Penny came back. In one hand she was carrying the basket in which she kept her toys. In the other, she had a doll blanket.

"Look, little dog," she said. "Here is a nice bed for you."

Setting the basket on the floor, she folded the blanket neatly and put it inside the basket. Cocking his head to one side, the little dog walked over to the basket. Sniff, sniff, sniff, went his little black nose. Then he walked around the basket, with his nose going sniff, sniff, sniff all the time.

Next, wagging his tail as hard as it could go, he climbed into the basket. Around and around and around he went. Then he lay down. But only for a minute. Up he jumped then to go around and around and around once more. Then he lay down again. But he didn't shut his eyes.

"That's the way dogs always go to bed," Roddy said. "They go around and around first."

Penny held her hand over the edge of the basket.

The little dog put his nose on her fingers and went sniff, sniff, sniff again.

"Sniff, sniff, sniff," said Penny.

"Hey, that's a keen name," said Ricky, coming into the kitchen in dry clothes. "Let's call him Sniff. What do you think, Rod?"

"Sure, let's call him Sniff," agreed Roddy.

"Sniff, Sniff, Sniff," echoed Penny.

2 6

That night, when Daddy drove his car into the garage, the twins and Penny were waiting for him on the back porch steps. With them was a little black dog whose tail was going wag, wag, wag.

"What's all this?" asked Daddy, getting out of his car and looking down at the little dog.

"That's Sniff," shouted Penny.

"That's Sniff," shouted the twins. "May we keep him, Daddy? Please!"

"Where did he come from?" asked Daddy.

At that, Ricky and Roddy and Penny all started talking.

"Hey, wait a minute," interrupted Daddy. "One at a time!"

First Roddy, then Ricky, then Penny told him how Joe had given the little dog to Roddy to look after, how Penny had thought of using her toy basket for the little dog's bed, and how the three of them together had named him Sniff.

"Mother says we must try to find his owner," Roddy added. "But if no one comes for him, please may we keep him, Daddy?"

"Mother is right," said Daddy. "We certainly

must try to find the person to whom he belongs. Isn't that what you would want to have happen if you had a little dog and he got lost?"

The twins considered it. "Y-y-yes," answered Ricky slowly. "All right, Daddy, we'll try to find his owner."

"Don't try so very hard," begged Penny. "I want this little black dog. You could buy the little boy or the little girl he belongs to another dog, couldn't you, Daddy? Then we could keep Sniff."

Daddy rumpled his small daughter's hair. "I'm afraid that wouldn't do," he said. "But for tonight, he's here. And if his owner does come for him, I'll tell you what I'll do. I'll get you another little black dog, as much as possible like this one."

"Thank you, Daddy," said Ricky and Roddy.

"Thank you, Daddy," said Penny.

But all three of them knew that there wasn't another little black dog in the world as nice as this one.

"Yap, yap," barked Sniff, just as though he agreed with them.

WATCHING AND WAITING

Next morning, as soon as Daddy had gone to work, Mother, three worried children, and one little black dog drove to the garage in the family car. Joe was outside, busily polishing. When he saw them, he put down his rag and came over to them.

"I guess you're wondering if anyone has showed up for this little dog," he said. "Nope. Nobody's been here and nobody's called. And Mike, over at the station, hasn't had any calls that I know of. That is, he hadn't when I stopped by last night. And he hasn't phoned me this morning."

"Goody!" shouted Ricky.

"Goody!" shouted Roddy.

"Goody, goody!" shouted Penny.

Joe grinned. "Looks like he's your dog, all right," he said.

But Mother told them, "Not so fast, children. Is Mike on duty at the Station this early in the day, Joe?"

Joe glanced at the clock above the garage door. "He's there by now, I guess," he said. "Come to think, he never gets there till around ten, though."

"I thought so," said Mother. "We'll have to go over to see Mr. Mike. Thank you, Joe." And she drove with Ricky and Roddy and Penny who were once more very worried, and with a little black dog who wasn't worried at all.

When they walked into the Police Station with Roddy carrying a wriggly little dog, sure enough, their friend, Mr. Mike, was just hanging up his hat.

"Good morning, all," said Mr. Mike in his cheerful voice. Then, looking down, he added, "But why the sad faces?"

"It's on account of Sniff," explained Roddy. "You see, we want to keep him."

"Yes, we want to keep him," said Ricky.

"Yes, we want to keep him," echoed Penny.

"Did anyone call about him while you were off duty?" asked Mother. "Joe said you didn't receive any inquiries last evening."

Mr. Mike looked at a book on the desk, then shook his head. "No, no calls this morning about a dog. What's more, none of the other boys has ever seen a puppy like this around town. And I haven't, either."

"Goody, goody," the twins and Penny started to say.

But Mr. Mike held up his hand. "Don't start celebrating for a while yet, children," he told them. "If the person who owns this dog lives at a distance, it'll take some time for him to get around to calling here. We always keep a dog a week before we decide he's probably lost. Then we call the Animal Rescue League to come and get him."

Mr. Mike grinned, then went on, "All of us here are kind of partial to dogs, you see. That's why we look after all the strays ourselves for a week. That's long enough to be pretty sure that the owner's not coming."

Just then the phone rang. Penny started to cry, and the twins looked as though they would like to.

In a moment, Mr. Mike put down the phone and said, "You're in luck so far. That was a lady who's lost her cat." Then he turned to Mother. "If it's all right with you, Mrs. Gray, the children may take the dog home and keep him until we see whether or not we can locate his owner."

Mother hesitated. "Every day he is with us, we will all love him more and more," she said. "Then if his owner does come, we'll be heartbroken if we have to give him up."

"I'd rather be heartbroken than not have Sniff for a while," declared Roddy.

"Me, too," said Ricky.

"Me, too," said Penny. Then she added, "And if his owner does come, I'll just give him all the pennies in my bank and tell him we're going to

33

keep Sniff and for him to go and buy himself another dog."

Mr. Mike threw back his head and laughed and laughed. "You sure have everything all figured out," he told Penny. "And I see you've named the dog, too."

Penny nodded. "We call him Sniff because he sniffs," he said.

Mr. Mike laughed again. "A very good reason for a very good name."

"Well, all right," said Mother. "We'll look after him. If you hear from his owner, give him our name, address, and phone number."

So Mother, Roddy, Ricky, and Penny and Sniff went out to the family car and drove back home.

Every day for a week, the twins and Penny were worried whenever they saw a stranger come down the street. They were worried when the phone rang. In fact, they were worried all the time. Daddy kept reminding them of his promise to buy them another dog, if Sniff's owner appeared. But that didn't make the children feel any better. They wanted Sniff.

And pretty soon, Mother and Daddy felt the same way. Sniff was such a lovable, happy little dog.

One morning, exactly a week after they had brought Sniff back from Mr. Mike's, the phone rang loudly. Penny and the twins were playing out in the yard. But when they heard the phone, they ran for the house. Mother was saying, "Hello," as they came in, and motioned for them to be still. Mother didn't do much talking. She just stood there saying, "Yes. Yes. I see."

The children grew more upset every minute. At last, Mother hung up the phone and turned toward them.

She was smiling happily. "I have good news for you—" she began. But she got no further. "He's ours," shouted the twins and Penny, all together. "Sniff belongs to us!"

Mother nodded. "Yes, we may keep Sniff. That was Mr. Mike to tell us they haven't had a single inquiry about him at the Station, and Joe hasn't, either. After all this time, they are sure no one will be coming after him."

It seemed to Ricky and Roddy and Penny, Sniff really understood that now he belonged to them. All that day his little tail went wag, wag, wag. And he romped and played with them just as though he were celebrating, too.

That night, when Daddy came home, he joined in the celebration. Then he said, "Now we can get organized. Tomorrow morning, you three children and Mother can take Sniff to the Tax Collector's office and get his dog license and tag. Of course, he'll need a collar, too. So after you have his license tag, go around to Mr. Locke's and buy a collar for him. Be sure to pick out one with a metal strip long enough to have his name and our telephone number marked on it. Then if he should stray off, any time, whoever picks him up will know where to call."

"About how much does a good collar cost?" asked Mother.

Daddy rubbed his chin. "I'm not sure," replied Daddy. "But that brings up something else. Do you know what I think, children? I think it would be a good plan for you to have a share in buying what Sniff needs."

Ricky and Roddy and Penny waited for Daddy to go on.

"It's this way," continued Daddy. "Sniff belongs to all of us. It's our job to look after him, in every way. And that includes buying what he needs. Well, your mother and I will see that he has plenty to eat and a nice home. We will buy the dog license and tag, too. How about you helping to buy his collar?"

Ricky looked at Roddy, and Roddy looked at Ricky.

"I've been saving up for a new bat," said Roddy.

"And I need a new bell for my bike," said Ricky. "But there isn't enough for that yet in my bank."

"And I don't have any money at all," added Penny. "Only just enough to buy new shoes for my doll."

They all laughed at that.

"You mean you don't have enough money for everything," said Roddy, importantly.

Roddy felt that he knew a great deal about money, and so did Ricky. They had had allowances for quite a long time, ten cents a week, each.

Daddy cleared his throat. "That's right, Roddy.

Very few people have money to buy everything they want at one time. So sensible people figure out what is most important to have and then buy that first. Your question now is, how important is Sniff?"

Ricky looked at Roddy again, and Roddy looked at Ricky. And both knew the answer. "Sniff!"

"All right," said Roddy, "I'll get my bank and see how much money I have."

"Me, too," said Ricky.

Penny looked down at Sniff. "Me, too," she said, and followed the boys upstairs.

A COLLAR FOR SNIFF

When Ricky came back, he had a pink pig bank in his hand. Grandmother Gray had given it to him when he was a little boy, and he had used it ever since. Roddy's pig from Grandmother was black and white. And Penny's bank was a white china rabbit.

The children sat down on the floor. Shake, shake, shake, shake went the banks, very fast.

"Yap," barked Sniff.

"He knows we're going to buy a collar for him,"
said Penny.

Shake, shake, shake—harder and faster, then still
harder and faster. Not a penny or a nickel or a dime
came out of either pig or the rabbit.

"Shake a little more slowly, children," said
Mother. "Then I think the money will come out."

40

Daddy put down his newspaper to watch.

Shake, shake, shake, very slowly. First a penny fell out of Ricky's pig, then one from Roddy's, then more and more, and nickels and dimes, too. Soon both boys had quite a little pile of money in front of them. But nothing had come from Penny's rabbit.

Penny began to cry. "I want to help buy Sniff his collar," she sobbed.

"Don't cry, Penny," said Roddy. "Give me your bank. I hear something clinking."

Roddy shook the white rabbit very slowly and two pennies rolled out.

"That's fine, Penny," said Ricky. "We'll give the rest."

But Ricky spoke too soon. When they counted up all the money, it came to only fifty-seven cents.

"Will fifty-seven cents buy a collar, Daddy?" Roddy asked anxiously.

Daddy shook his head. "I don't imagine so. But don't worry about that. Your mother and I will make up the difference. Fifty-seven cents is a good share for eight-year-old twins and a five-year-old little girl."

It was fun taking Sniff to the Tax Collector's office the next day and having Mother tell the man Sniff's and Daddy's names and their address. And they all liked the little license tag that Sniff was going to wear on his new collar.

"It is just like a locket," said Penny.

Then they went on to Mr. Locke's hardware store to buy the new collar. Sniff followed them right in, living up to his name by running all around, sniffing everything he could find.

It took a while to choose the collar, for Mr. Locke had so many pretty ones to sell. But at last they decided on a bright green one that seemed exactly right for a little black dog. And, sure enough, the green collar had a metal strip which Mr. Locke said gave plenty of room for Sniff's name and their telephone number.

"By any chance do you have any more shopping to do this morning, Mrs. Gray?" Mr. Locke asked then. "What I have in mind is that if you do, I could be attaching the license tag to the collar, and Mr. Watkins next door could do the engraving, too."

Mr. Watkins was a jeweler, and his store was next door to Mr. Locke's.

"Why, thank you, Mr. Locke," said Mother. "That would be fine."

"What's engraving?" asked Penny.

"It's putting the telephone number and Sniff's name on the metal strip," said Roddy.

"Oh," said Penny. "Is the metal strip part of my present to Sniff?"

"This collar is a present from all three children and from Mr. Gray and me, Mr. Locke," explained Mother. "Yes, Penny, the metal strip is part of your present."

"I advise having your name on it, too," suggested Mr. Locke. Then, to Sniff he said, "Now, then, young fellow, come here and see how your fine new collar fits."

Picking Sniff up from the floor and standing him on the counter, Mr. Locke fastened the green collar around Sniff's neck. It fitted beautifully.

"Pretty handsome, I'd say," said Mr. Locke.

But Sniff didn't act at all pleased with his present.

He shook his head from side to side, then scratched
at the collar.

"Stop, Sniff," said Mother sternly. "Stop it, I say."

"Yap!" barked Sniff.

"I guess that means he doesn't want to wear
a collar," said Penny.

"He'll get used to it," said Mr. Locke, taking the

44

collar off. "Almost all dogs fuss about wearing a collar when one is first put on them."

After the marketing was finished, they all went back to Mr. Locke's. Sure enough, the collar was ready. The license tag dangled from its ring. And on the metal strip in very clear letters was:

SNIFF

Call Gray — Center 786

SNIFF LEARNS GAMES AND TRICKS

That night, when Daddy came home, he thought
the green collar very fine indeed. And he agreed
with Mr. Locke that in time Sniff would get used
to it.

He certainly wasn't used to it yet. He scratched
and scratched and scratched at it, until Mother took
him up on her lap and held his little paws.

"Can we teach Sniff to do tricks?" asked Penny.

"Sure we can," the twins told her, scornfully.
"What do you think? He's a very smart dog."

"I wonder if he is as smart as my dog Sport was," said Daddy. "That bell trick of Sport's was a good one."

Daddy had told the twins and Penny many stories about Sport, the dog he had when he was a boy. But this was the first time he had ever mentioned any bell trick.

"What was the bell trick, Daddy?" they asked. "Tell us."

"Well," Daddy began, "we kept a bell on the floor beside the back door, and whenever Sport wanted to go outdoors, he would ring it. I don't know who had the idea of teaching him to do it. But it certainly worked."

Daddy paused a moment, then said to Mother, "Say, isn't that bell up in the attic somewhere? It seems to me I remember seeing it the last time we cleaned up there."

"If it's the bell I think it is, I know right where to look," said Mother, putting Sniff down and jumping up from her chair. "I'll go see."

Sure enough, in a little while Mother came back

with an old-fashioned bell in her hand. The bell was quite large and had a long handle.

"That's it," said Daddy. "My grandfather gave it to me, and he always said it was the kind of bell his schoolteacher used at his school, to call the children in from recess."

"Show us how Sport rang it," said Roddy.

48

So they all went to the back door, and Daddy stood the bell on the floor.

"You can't say that Sport rang it, exactly," he explained. "He used to bat it over with his paw, then push it with his nose and send it rolling. That made a fine, loud noise and whoever heard it would come and let Sport out."

"Come on, Sniff," said Ricky. "Ring the bell."

But Sniff didn't like the bell one bit. He backed away from it, growling fiercely.

"He's frightened of it," said Mother. "Don't try to make him do anything with it now, children. Let him get used to it. We'll leave it here beside the door, and by and by he will know it isn't anything to be scared of.

"Anyway," Mother went on, "I don't think the time has come to teach Sniff any tricks. Let's just play with him for a while. He will love that, I'm sure."

So that is what the twins and Penny did. And Mother was right. Sniff loved to play. He played all the time he wasn't eating or sleeping. Whenever he was alone, he went right on. He played with his tail, which he could never quite catch, no matter how hard he tried. He played ball. He even played dolls if he could get at them and Penny didn't come in to stop him.

But Sniff didn't like to be alone. The family discovered that when they first shut him up in the kitchen for the night. Sniff fussed and scratched the kitchen door and barked and barked. That is, he did for three nights. Then, just as though he knew it was no use to fuss, he quieted down.

"He's smart, all right," Daddy said. "When he sees he isn't getting anywhere, he gives up. That's a good thing for children as well as dogs to know."

Every morning, as soon as the twins were dressed, they rushed down to the kitchen. There was Sniff, his paws over the edge of his basket, his brown eyes watching them eagerly.

But he didn't move until Roddy or Ricky said, "Hi, Sniff!"

That was the signal. With a leap, Sniff was out of the basket and upon them, jumping and barking in excitement. Then he would run around the kitchen like mad until the boys opened the back door. Out Sniff would dash into the yard then, still barking.

Because it was summertime, Mother would put his bowl of milk and cornflakes on the back porch. And by the time the family had eaten their breakfast, Sniff was ready to go places.

He loved running races with Penny and her friend, Susan, and Susan's big dog, Wolf. Sniff was so little and his legs were so short that he couldn't help falling down every so often, and rolling over and over. Sometimes he rolled in front of Wolf, and it looked as though Wolf would fall down on top of him. But Wolf would always skid to a stop, then step very carefully over his small friend.

Then up Sniff would jump, and off the two dogs would go yapping and barking as hard as they could. Pretty soon, there Sniff would be again, down on the ground and rolling over and over. But he never seemed to mind his tumbles.

Sniff thought the boys' ball-game was lots of fun, too. They played that with Jock and David down the block, and with Rex and Sunny, Jock's and David's dogs. It was a game of catch, and whenever

one of the boys missed, Sniff and Rex and Sunny tore after the ball. Most of the time either Rex or Sunny got the ball and brought it back to the boys. But once in a while, Sniff won and, picking the ball up in his mouth, would take it to Roddy or Ricky.

He did one thing, though, that neither Rex nor Sunny did. Whenever he decided he was too tired to play any more, he would lie flat down on the ground, wherever he was, and go to sleep. Sometimes Rex and Sunny would run over to him and push at him with their noses. But Sniff didn't open his eyes. He went right on sleeping until he was ready to play again.

It was another matter when the twins started for home. Up Sniff would jump then, wide awake, and dash after them.

One Saturday, Daddy said, "I think the time has come for us to start teaching Sniff some tricks. He learns so fast, it won't take long."

"What tricks?" asked Roddy, very carefully not mentioning the bell.

Sniff still hated that bell. Whenever he wanted to go outdoors, he would go to the back door and yap. But he kept as far as possible from the bell. Sometimes, he growled at it fiercely. No, Roddy wasn't going to mention the bell trick, and neither was Ricky. They didn't want to give Daddy a chance to remind them how much smarter Sport had been.

To their relief, Daddy didn't. "What tricks?" Roddy repeated.

"Well, I think we should start with what he does naturally. Something he is already doing, only we'll tie it up to a trick."

"He rolls on the ground all the time when he's playing with Susan and Wolf and me," said Penny.

"The very thing," exclaimed Daddy. "We'll start with that."

"He brings back the ball to us when we play catch," said Ricky.

"That is, he does when he can get it or when he isn't sleeping," added Roddy.

"Excellent," said Daddy. "The word for that is 'fetch.' Now let's see how smart he really is."

Sniff certainly was a smart little dog. In no time at all, he was rolling over when they said, "Roll, Sniff." He was running after a stick as well as the ball, when they said, "Fetch, Sniff." Pretty soon he was sitting down when they said, "Sit." And he was standing up on his hind legs and barking when he was hungry.

"Why don't we try him with the bell again?" Daddy suggested to the twins one evening.

Penny was over at Susan's, for which Ricky and Roddy were thankful. They didn't want her to see what was going to happen now. Slowly they followed Daddy and Mother out to the back door, Sniff at their heels, as usual.

Daddy squatted down on the floor and held out the bell to Sniff. "Come on, little fellow," he coaxed. "It won't hurt you."

Sniff didn't move.

"Look, Sniff," said Daddy patiently, putting the bell down on the floor. "This is all you have to do." And Daddy knocked the bell over.

Sniff didn't move.

"Now, Sniff," said Daddy, very firmly now. "Come here. I want you to try it."

When Sniff didn't move this time either, Daddy reached over and pulled Sniff to him. Then, picking up one of Sniff's paws, he knocked over the bell with it.

Sniff pulled his paw from Daddy's hand, turned around, and lay down on the floor. Then he closed his eyes.

Daddy chuckled. "At least he knows when he's had enough," said Daddy, getting up from the floor and brushing off his trousers.

"And I've had enough, too," declared Mother. "I hadn't intended to say anything about this now, but I guess I'll have to. I think, the time has come to be very strict with Sniff about his chewing. Last week, it was your new bedroom slipper, Daddy. This morning, it was Penny's doll. He just about ruined it, and I don't blame Penny for crying."

Daddy looked down at Sniff, sleeping peacefully on the floor. "Yes," he agreed. "The time has certainly come to do something about that chewing. We'll start tomorrow."

SNIFF CHEWS

The very next morning, Sniff chewed up his pretty green collar. There it was, on the floor of the porch, when the twins went out after breakfast.

"I guess he must have worked it loose in some way," said Daddy, when the twins took him out to see what Sniff had done. "Then he went to work on it, all right. He never liked it, and this was his chance. Well, that is that."

Then, "Come here, Sniff," Daddy called.

Sniff came running. Daddy sat down on the porch

steps, the ruined collar in his hand. Pulling Sniff
over to him, he put Sniff's nose on the chewed-up
collar and said, "Bad dog, Sniff. Bad, bad, dog."

Sniff understood the tone of Daddy's voice, all
right, for he looked very sad. And because Daddy
kept holding his nose against the collar, he realized
that a collar was not for chewing. At least, that is
what the family decided later.

Just then, Jock and David began whistling and
calling for the boys to come and play catch.

"Go along and have your fun," said Daddy to
Ricky and Roddy. "This afternoon will be plenty
of time to go and buy a new collar. Meanwhile, I'll
get the pliers and take the dog tag off this one."

Ricky and Roddy didn't move.

"We haven't very much money," said Ricky.

"Oh, that," said Daddy. "I don't think you children should pay for the new collar. We'll call it a
happenstance, and Mother and I will buy it."

"What's a happenstance?" asked Penny.

"It's something that just happens and isn't anyone's fault. Run along and play now, children. I've
got to mow the lawn."

Penny went over to Susan's. And Sniff, deciding
he preferred a game of catch, raced down the street
after the twins. The four boys and three dogs had
a glorious game, and before they knew it, it was
time for lunch.

On the way home, David asked, "Why isn't Sniff wearing his collar?"

"He got it off some way and chewed it up," answered Ricky. "We're going to buy him a new one this afternoon. But I wish we didn't have to."

"Why?" asked David.

"Because he doesn't like to wear a collar," Ricky told him.

"He's fussed at it ever since we bought it," added Roddy.

"Well, you'd better get him another right away," said David. "It's bad to let your dog run around without a collar and his tag."

"Sniff stays right with us," said Ricky. "He doesn't run around."

David shook his head. "That doesn't make any difference. Besides, it's the law that every dog should have his tax tag on, all the time. And you never can tell. Sniff might run away and get lost, sometime when you're not looking. He's awfully curious, always poking his nose into everything."

The twins did not answer. They were remembering how Sniff had been lost when Joe found him.

"I guess you're right," said Ricky, at last. "Anyway, we're going after a new collar right after lunch."

As they were finishing lunch, their next-door neighbor, Mrs. Snyder, called up to see if Mother would help her with a quilt that afternoon. And a man phoned Daddy to ask if he could come over for a business talk.

"Your mother will have to take you to buy the new collar Monday afternoon, I guess," said Daddy.

"But, Daddy," said Ricky, "David says it's against the law to let a dog run around without his dog tax tag. We can't keep Sniff cooped up all the time until Monday."

"That's right," agreed Daddy. "Well, why don't you children walk downtown to Mr. Locke's? It's a pretty long walk, but it won't hurt you any."

Taking out his wallet, he said, "Here's a dollar. If the collar costs more, tell Mr. Locke I'll stop by on Monday to pay him the rest. Be sure to get one that fastens firmly."

Ricky put the money in his pocket, and he and Roddy and Penny and Sniff started off. If Mother hadn't been hurrying to get over to Mrs. Snyder's, and if Daddy hadn't had his mind on business, one of them would have remembered about the tag on the porch table. As for Ricky and Roddy and Penny, they were so excited about going downtown alone, they completely forgot to take the tag along.

Mother called after them, "Come straight home as soon as you have bought the collar."

"We will," promised the children.

When they at last walked into Mr. Locke's store again, Penny announced, "We've come to buy a collar for Sniff."

Mr. Locke looked down at the little black dog who was following right along. "A collar! But you bought one just the other day. What happened?"

"Sniff got it off some way and then chewed it up," explained Ricky.

"And Daddy says to be sure to get a new one that will stay fastened," added Roddy.

"My, my," said Mr. Locke, leaning over the counter and talking to Sniff. "It's bones that are meant for chewing, not collars."

Sniff wagged his tail and barked, "Yap!"

Penny giggled. Then, shaking her finger at Sniff, she repeated, "It's bones that are meant for chewing, not collars."

"Oh, Penny," said Roddy. And Penny giggled again.

Mr. Locke took a big box down from the shelf. "I recommend one of these," he said, opening the box. "See, they have brass studs on them. If a dog does manage to get one of these collars off, he won't do much chewing because the studs will hurt his teeth."

"That's a good idea," said Roddy.

"I like those studs," said Penny. "They're pretty."

"But I must tell you that this kind of collar costs twenty-five cents more than the other you bought," Mr. Locke told them.

"Daddy said to get a good one," said Ricky, taking the dollar bill from his pocket. "But this is all the money we have with us."

"That's all right," replied Mr. Locke. "Your dad can stop in and pay me the rest sometime when he's going by."

"He said he would come down on Monday with the rest of the money, if it cost more," said Roddy, remembering.

"Fine," said Mr. Locke. "Now then, which color do you prefer?"

Just then Penny spied a collar with a bell on it. "Let's get that one," she said. "It would be lots of fun for Sniff to have a bell on his collar."

Ricky shook his head. "Dogs don't have bells on their collars. Bells are for cats, so that they can't catch birds."

Penny changed her mind. "Sniff doesn't like bells, anyway," she said.

So they all looked at the collars in the box—the brown one and the black one and the red one and the green one. Mr. Locke told them the brown and black ones wouldn't get dirty as quickly as the others. And the children decided against the green one because Sniff never had liked his other collar. That left black, brown, and red.

"I like red best," declared Penny. "It's lots prettier than brown or black."

The twins thought so, too.

"Now, then," said Mr. Locke, "give me Sniff's dog tax tag and I'll put it on right away."

The dog tax tag! They had forgotten to bring it.

"That's too bad," said Mr. Locke. "I never like to see a dog go out without his tag. And Mr. Watkins isn't in his store today. So he can't engrave Sniff's name on this collar, and your phone number, as he did before. Well, we'll put the red collar on, anyway, and as soon as you get home, your Daddy can fasten on the tag. Here, Sniff! Come and get your new collar."

Sniff was at the back of the store, sniffing at a big box.

"Come, Sniff," Mr. Locke called again.

"Come, Sniff," called Roddy.

Sniff came running. Penny sat down on the floor and took him on her lap. "Let me put his new collar on," she said.

Mr. Locke handed it down to her, and, taking it up in her hand, Penny held it in front of Sniff's nose. "Look, Sniff," she said. "Here is a nice new collar for you. It is very pretty, don't you think?"

To the twins' surprise, Sniff didn't wiggle and twist while Penny put the red collar on. And when she had fastened it carefully, he didn't fuss or scratch it.

"You're a good dog," Roddy told him, leaning over to pat him.

"You sure are a good dog," said Ricky, rubbing Sniff behind his ears.

Sniff knew what "good" meant. Wag, wag, wag went his little tail. And "Yap!" he barked.

"I guess he does like red better than he did green," said Penny, as they went out the door.

"Keep your eye on him all the way home," called Mr. Locke. "Don't let him out of your sight for a second."

WHERE IS SNIFF?

The children and Sniff had walked only a half block toward home, when a fire engine came clanging down the street.

"It's a fire!" shouted Roddy.

"Yap, yap," barked Sniff in excitement.

He liked that big red thing that was going so fast. Maybe this was a new kind of game! In an instant, Sniff took off after the engine.

"Sniff is going to the fire," cried Ricky. "Come on. We'll go, too."

And pell-mell the three of them raced after Sniff, forgetting they had promised Mother to come straight home from Mr. Locke's store. The fire was in a large, empty building two blocks away. Roddy and Ricky and Penny got there in no time, catching up with Sniff on the way.

It was all very exciting. The firemen took hoses from their truck and connected them to a hydrant. Other firemen lifted ladders from another truck and put them up against the burning building. Mr. Mike was there, too, with several other policemen, keeping the crowd of people a safe distance away from the fire and from the firemen so that they could do their work properly.

Very quickly, streams of water began shooting out of the hose onto the flames that were coming out of the windows up near the roof. And it was so thrilling to watch that the twins and Penny forgot all about Sniff.

At first, Sniff, too, thought the fire exciting. He ran around and around, barking and investigating.

But when a fireman shouted at him, angrily,

"Hey you, dog. Get out of here," Sniff decided it was time to go back to his own folks.

But where were they? Not anywhere that Sniff could see. All he could find were lots and lots of strange people. And there was so much noise that soon he began to feel very, very tired.

Tired! Sniff stopped where he was and lay down in the middle of the street.

It was good that a kind man came along just then. Leaning over Sniff, he picked him up. "Where is your master, little dog?" the man asked gently. "You mustn't sleep here in the street. You'll get run over."

Then, putting the squirming Sniff down once more, he commanded, "Go home, little dog. Go home!"

Sniff knew what "home" meant. But where was home? Whirling around, he ran away as fast as he could go—right toward the fire.

The kind man looked after him. "I shouldn't have let him loose," he said to himself. "His dog tag would have showed me to whom he belonged."

In a moment, Sniff came to a red car. It was the

same size as Daddy's and the door was open. Sniff jumped in and hopped up onto the seat. There, this was better!

The car belonged to the Fire Chief, who was off directing the firemen. And everyone around was so busy that no one noticed Sniff sitting bolt upright. He was looking and looking for Roddy and Ricky and Penny.

As soon as no more flames were coming out of the windows, the children remembered about Sniff.

"Here, Sniff! Come, Sniff," they called.

Sniff didn't answer. Nor could the children see him anywhere at all.

Very worried, Ricky and Roddy and Penny asked all the people nearby, "Have you seen a little black dog with a red collar?" No one had.

The children could see Mr. Mike over toward the burning building. But when they tried to go to him, another policeman stopped them.

"Anyone with you kids?" he asked.

The children shook their heads.

"Then you'd better go home fast," he said. "A fire's no place for kids alone."

"But we've lost our dog," said Ricky. "He's little and black and he has a red collar on."

"Don't worry," said the policeman, "anyone who finds him can locate you by his dog tag."

"But he hasn't—" began Ricky.

Just then, the policeman saw a boy trying to get through the lines. "Hey!" he called, and ran over to the boy.

"I guess we'd better go home," said Ricky.

"I think so, too," said Roddy. "Anyway, maybe Sniff has found his way back to the house by now. Come on, Penny."

Back in the Fire Chief's car, Sniff had settled down for a nap. If the car had not been so near the burning building, he might have heard the boys and Penny call him. As it was, he was out of everyone's way and very comfortable. So he slept on and on.

Three sad children walked slowly toward home, with Penny crying as though her heart would break. When they were a block and a half away from their house, they saw Mother and Daddy hurrying along.

"Where on earth have you been?" asked Daddy.

73

"What is the matter?" asked Mother.

"Sniff is lost," said the twins.

Penny threw herself into Mother's arms. "And we'll never see him again," she sobbed.

"The fire engines came by and we went to the fire," Roddy told them.

"And we forgot to watch Sniff," said Ricky.

"And he didn't have his dog tax tag on because we forgot it," added Roddy.

"Don't cry, Penny dear," said Mother. "Crying won't help. Probably Sniff was afraid of all the people and the excitement and is on his way home now. Dogs usually know how to get back home, you know."

"I'll go get my car and run around to the Police Station," said Daddy. "Sniff may have been turned in there."

Mother and the three children went on home. No little black dog was anywhere around. And when Daddy came back, no little black dog was with him.

"Nobody has called up the Station to say he's

been found," Daddy told them. "All we can do now is wait."

None of them wanted to look at television that evening. Nobody wanted to talk about anything but Sniff. When it was bedtime, and Sniff still hadn't come back, the twins and Penny went sadly upstairs.

Long after Penny was asleep in her room, the twins were still awake.

"Do you think Sniff ran away because he didn't like us any more?" asked Roddy. "Or maybe because he didn't want to wear a collar?"

"No, I don't think so," replied Ricky. "He just got excited, the way we did."

Neither twin spoke for a few minutes, then Ricky asked, "Why didn't Mother or Daddy scold us about not coming straight home?"

At that, Mother came into the room and Roddy asked her.

"No, we didn't scold you," she said softly. "Daddy and I knew you would realize why Sniff was lost. It was because you didn't keep your promise about coming straight home."

"I wish we had kept it," said Ricky.

"I do, too," said Roddy.

Mother leaned over each twin, and kissed him. "I do, too," she told them. "Now go to sleep, boys. We will find Sniff tomorrow, I'm sure."

SNIFF RINGS THE BELL

Next morning, three very quiet children had a hard time eating their breakfast. At first they had told Mother they didn't want to eat anything. But both Daddy and Mother said they must or they couldn't hunt for Sniff. So they did their best with the orange juice, oatmeal, and toast and milk.

"Where shall we look first, Daddy?" Ricky asked, wiping his mouth.

"I think the first thing is for me to run down to the Police Station and see if anyone has reported

78

finding a black Scottie answering to the name of Sniff," Daddy told them. "I'd take you along, but it will be better for you to stay right here, in case he comes straight home."

So Ricky and Roddy and Penny sat on the front steps and watched. Before long, there was Daddy's car coming back. He was waving his hand out the car window, and as he came nearer, they could see he was smiling.

And what was that jumping around on the seat beside him? It was! It was! It was Sniff! The minute Daddy opened the car door, Sniff was out, running to them, jumping up on them and barking and barking.

"Sniff's home!" shouted Penny, hopping up and down.

"Sniff's home!" shouted Ricky, turning a somersault.

"Sniff's home!" shouted Roddy, doing a handspring.

"Yap, yap, yap, yap," barked Sniff.

Mother came running. "Oh, Sniff," she cried. And Sniff ran swiftly to jump up on her, too.

"Where on earth did you find him?" Mother asked, as soon as she could catch her breath.

"Where was he, Daddy?" shouted the children.

"You'll never guess!" replied Daddy. "You know the Fire House is just this side of the Police Station. Well, I was driving along slowly, thinking I might catch sight of Sniff along the way, when what should I see but Chief Davis coming out of the Fire House door with a little dog in his arms. I pulled up and got out, thinking the little dog might be Sniff. I had taken only a few steps, when the dog began to bark and struggle to get out of the Chief's arms. I knew then that it was Sniff, all right.

"When I came up beside the Chief, he was laughing. 'There's no doubt about whose dog this is, Mr. Gray,' he said.

"I took Sniff in my arms, but he was so excited I had to put him down so that he could race around and around me, barking all the while."

"How did Chief Davis get Sniff?" asked Roddy.

"Well, it seems that when the Chief went back to his car after the fire was out yesterday afternoon, there was Sniff, fast asleep on the seat. There wasn't any tag on his collar, of course, and no one any-where about had seen him before. It was pretty late by that time, so Chief Davis decided the best thing to do was to take the little lost dog back to the Fire House for the night. When I came along, the Chief was starting for the Police Station to turn Sniff over to Mr. Mike. All the firemen fell in love with Sniff, the Chief told me. They thought he was one of the cutest little pups they had ever seen."

"Sure he is," said Ricky.

"I guess we'd better put his dog tag on right away quick," said Roddy.

"I think so, too," said Daddy.

Daddy got out his pliers, and they all went out on the back porch.

"You take the new collar off, Roddy," said Daddy. "It's a pretty one, isn't it, with those studs?"

"We forgot to tell you, Daddy," said Ricky. "It cost a dollar and a quarter."

"I'll stop in and give Mr. Locke the extra quarter tomorrow," said Daddy.

"I will do it the first thing in the morning," said Mother. "I'd like to get that engraving done as soon as possible."

When Roddy unfastened the collar, Sniff didn't fuss a bit.

"Look, Sniff," Roddy said then. "This nice red collar with all the brass studs belongs to you." And he held the collar out to Sniff.

Sniff looked at the collar, sniffed at it, then reached out a paw and patted it.

"He likes it," cried Penny. "I think it's the studs."

After Daddy had put the dog tag on, Sniff stood still without wriggling while Roddy fastened the red collar back on. And he didn't scratch at it at all when he jumped down for another romp.

"I guess he likes red better than green, all right," said Ricky.

"I'm going to watch him every minute until Mr. Watkins puts his name and our phone number on the metal strip," declared Ricky.

"I am, too," said Roddy.

"I am, too," said Penny.

But watching Sniff every minute wasn't easy. He was still so excited and happy about being home again that he rushed here and there and everywhere. At last the children decided to shut him in the house, so that they could play a game of hide-and-seek until it was time to get dressed for Sunday school.

Sniff didn't like that a bit. It was much too quiet indoors. Mother was upstairs, writing a letter to Grandmother Gray. Daddy had gone out on an errand. All the rooms seemed very large and empty to the little dog.

Out in the kitchen once more, he could hear Ricky and Roddy and Penny laughing and shouting. That was where he wanted to be!

"Yap, yap, yap," he barked by the door. No one came to open it.

Then he tried the kitchen window. He was too small to get his paws up on the sill, but he jumped as high as he could, and barked as loudly as he could. No one came. Sniff became very angry. This was a fine way to treat a fellow!

Whirling around, he spied the bell by the kitchen

door. That horrid thing! He'd show it! Rushing over, with a swoop he knocked the bell down. Then, getting his teeth into the handle, he shook and shook it. Ring, ring, ring, went the bell.

Mother heard it, all the way upstairs. Putting down her fountain pen, she ran down. Sniff was still shaking the bell. Mother couldn't help laughing at the comical sight. Then she opened the kitchen door.

"Come quickly, children," she called. "Sniff is ringing the bell."

Ricky and Roddy and Penny came running. Sniff didn't stop even when he saw them beside him.

Ring, ring, ring, the bell kept going.

"He had the handle in his teeth and he was ringing it just that way when I came downstairs," Mother told them.

Sniff dropped the bell then, and looking up wagged his tail. "Yap," he barked.

"Good Sniff," said Ricky.

"Good Sniff," said Roddy and Penny. And they all patted him.

Sniff liked it all. He liked being called good. He liked the attention he was getting.

"See if he will do it again," suggested Mother.

So Ricky sat down on the floor, and, holding the handle of the bell out to Sniff, said, "Here, Sniff, good dog. Ring the bell again."

Sniff looked at Ricky. He looked up at Mother. He looked at the bell. And he took the handle between his teeth and rang the bell for all he was worth.

"When Daddy comes home, he'll have to say Sniff is as smart as Sport was," declared Ricky.

"He will if Sniff does it again," said Roddy.

That was exactly what Daddy did say, for Sniff rang the bell when they told him to, just as though he had always done it. As for the new red collar, he liked that, too. Not once did he ever fuss about it, or scratch at it. And when he wanted to go out he always rang the bell!

THE END